For my big sister, who loves otters—N. B.
For Jenny—A. Z.

union square kids
NEW YORK

UNION SQUARE KIDS and the distinctive Union Square Kids logo are registered trademarks of Union Square & Co., LLC.

Union Square & Co., LLC, is a subsidiary of Sterling Publishing Co., Inc.

Text © 2023 Nelly Buchet
Illustrations © 2023 Andrea Zuill

ISBN 978-1-4549-4452-2

Library of Congress Cataloging-in-Publication Data

Names: Buchet, Nelly, author. | Zuill, Andrea, illustrator.

Title: A friend like no otter / by Nelly Buchet ; illustrated by Andrea Zuill.

Description: New York : Union Square Kids, [2023] | Audience: Ages 4-8. | Summary: Otter loves playing with her pet rock, Rock, and one day Manatee joins Otter and Rock, but disaster strikes which threatens Otter and Manatee's friendship.

Identifiers: LCCN 2022032810 | ISBN 9781454944522 (hardcover)

Subjects: CYAC: Friendship--Fiction. | Forgiveness--Fiction. | Otters--Fiction. | Manatees--Fiction. | LCGFT: Picture Books.

Classification: LCC PZ7.1.B818 Fr 2023 | DDC [E]--dc23

LC record available at https://lccn.loc.gov/2022032810

For information about custom editions, special sales, and premium purchases, please contact specialsales@unionsquareandco.com.

Printed in China

Lot #:
2 4 6 8 10 9 7 5 3 1

01/23

unionsquareandco.com

Cover and interior design by Gina Bonanno

A Friend Like No Otter

by Nelly Buchet * illustrated by Andrea Zuill

union
square
kids

NEW YORK

Otter has a pet rock.
She takes Rock everywhere—
when she dives underwater
or floats on her back
for a fat catnap.

Rock doesn't mind.

Otter plays with Rock.
She dresses Rock in sea slug hats,

purple seaweed skirts,

and seashell necklaces.
Rock doesn't mind.

Otter takes care of Rock.
She scrubs and gives sea-foam baths so Rock sparkles like the waves
churning and crashing in the surf.

Rock doesn't mind.

At the end of the day,
when the sun goes down
and the ocean gets quiet,
Otter whispers her dreams to Rock.
Things that make her happy, or sad,
or somewhere in between.

Rock doesn't mind.

Then she tucks Rock in her pocket.

The one in her armpit where she keeps special things, like rocks, that don't talk, but listen.

Manatee doesn't have a pet rock.
Having one looks like fun.
She watches Otter and Rock splashing,
giggling, juggling.
She'd like to play.

Rock wouldn't mind.

Otter isn't so sure.

But Manatee makes seagrass hair for Rock.
And Otter can't say no to a present.
Even if green really isn't Rock's color.

Rock doesn't mind.

Otter and Manatee play with Rock.

They tickle Rock with their whiskers,

balance Rock on their noses,

and tell jokes only they think are funny.

Rock doesn't mind.

Manatee throws a fast one.
Otter takes a swing.
It's a home run!
Rock goes sailing.

Higher than Dolphin can jump,
faster than Seagull can dive,
farther than Whale is long.

Rock doesn't mind.
But Otter does!

Manatee pushes her tail into the waves, paddling as fast as she can.
She reaches with her flipper, stretching so far she shakes.
She misses Rock by an inch.
Manatee swims in circles, calling for Rock, looking underwater.

But Rock is gone.

Otter wishes she'd never shared Rock,
who would be safe in her pocket, the one in her armpit
where she keeps special things, like rocks, that don't talk,
but listen.

Manatee panics. It's all her fault.

If only she'd caught Rock.
If only she hadn't asked to play.

If only she'd left Otter alone.

Manatee has to do something!

Otter won't talk to her
and she won't listen.
Manatee has to fix this.
She has to find Rock,
at the bottom of the ocean.

But she can't breathe underwater.
She can't hold her breath forever.

So Manatee calls over Seagull,

who asks Whale

to talk to Eel,

who gets through to Crab,

who asks Frogfish
if she's heard the news.

But Frogfish doesn't notice anything unusual.
She doesn't see the small, shiny rock
dropping deeper and deeper
and deeper down to the ocean floor.
Frogfish can't see Rock land at the bottom, in the sand,
where it's soft, and quiet, and dark . . .

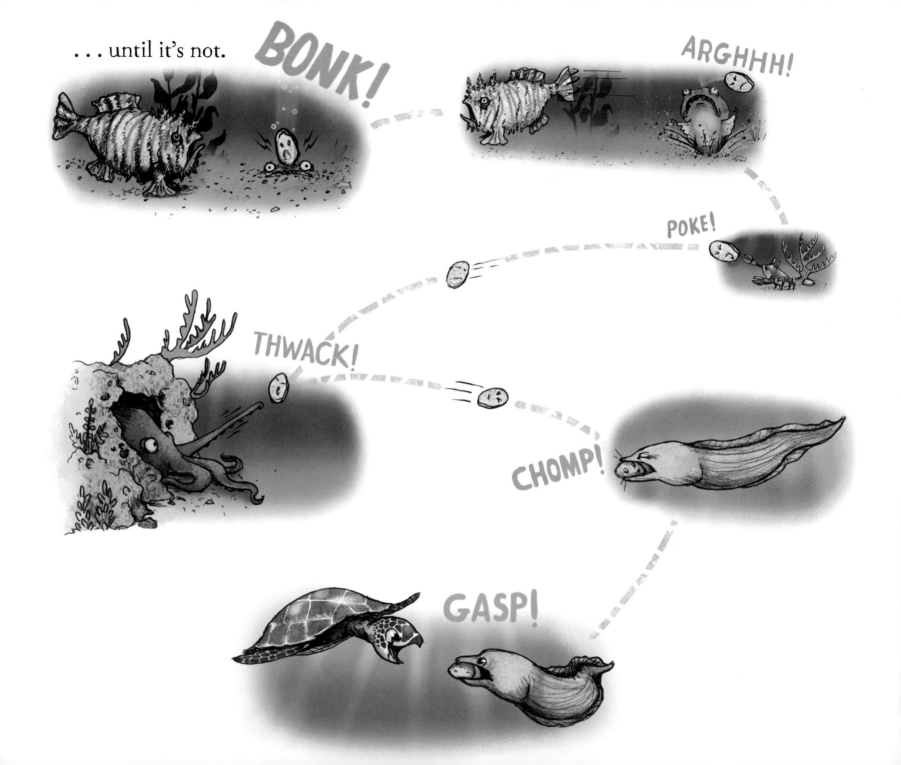

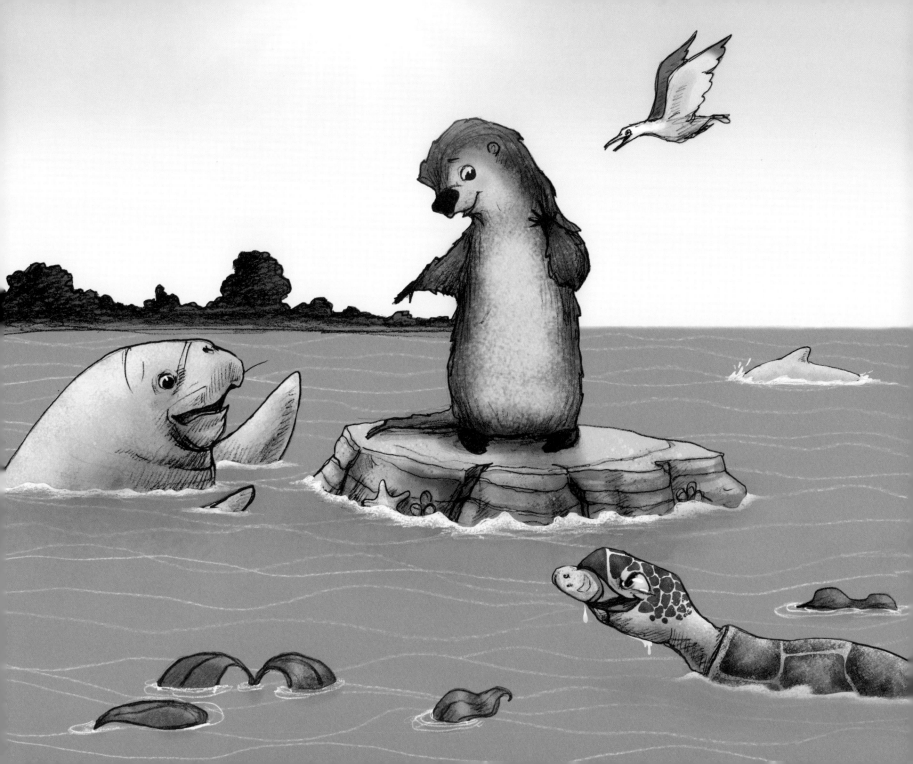

Otter has a pet rock.
It's more fun to play with Rock
when Manatee's around.

They do everything together.
And sometimes, they share Rock with others.

Rock doesn't mind.

Author's Note

Otters really do have pet rocks. Manatees don't, but they do live in the southwestern Atlantic Ocean around Florida and the Caribbean Sea.

Both otters and manatees are marine animals. They're super swimmers, but they can't breathe underwater like fish. Otters keep their heads out of the water most of the time, but manatees only poke out their noses to breathe. This happens every four to five minutes, except when they sleep. Manatees sink to the bottom, like Rock, and can rest for twenty minutes in their bed of seagrass before needing air.

Otters do the opposite when sleeping: They float on the surface and hold hands with their family to stay together. Sadly, the fact that otters and manatees live so close to us on the surface of the water makes them vulnerable to motorized water vehicles. They get hurt very badly by people who forget they are just visitors in Otter and Manatee's home. The animals also suffer because of human-caused pollution, which makes for an imbalanced ecosystem. If you'd like to help your community protect the environment, check out local volunteer organizations that are doing important work restoring wildlife habitats.